To Ella
who is a beautiful
butterfly

tiger tales
an imprint of ME Media, LLC
202 Old Ridgefield Road, Wilton, CT 06897
Published in the United States 2005
Originally published in Great Britain 2004
By Little Tiger Press
An imprint of Magi Publications
Text and illustrations copyright © 2004 Liz Pichon
Library of Congress Cataloging-in-Publication Data

Pichon, Liz.
  The very ugly bug / by Liz Pichon.
     p. cm.
  Summary: A bug is so ugly she scares away the bird
that was about to devour her.
  ISBN 1-58925-048-6 (hardcover)
  [1. Insects—Fiction. 2. Ugliness—Fiction.] I. Title.
  PZ7.P5555Ve 2005
                                        2004017277

ISBN 1-59825-048-6
Printed in Spain
1 3 5 7 9 10 8 6 4 2

The Very Ugly Bug

by Liz Pichon

tiger tales

There was once an ugly bug.
A **very** ugly bug.

She had huge googly eyes,

a lumpy, wibbly-wobbly head,

a horrible hairy back,

and spotted purple legs.

What a sight she was!

The very ugly bug wondered why the
other bugs didn't look like her.

"Spotty red bug, why are your eyes
so teeny tiny, and not big and googly
like mine?"

"My eyes are teeny tiny so I can
hide in the berries and be safe from
birds," said the spotty red bug.

"Skinny green bug, why is your back so smooth and green, and not hairy like mine?" asked the very ugly bug.

"My smooth green back means I can hide in the leaves and be safe from birds," said the skinny green bug.

"Shiny blue bug, why do you have such big fluttery wings? I don't have any wings at all," said the very ugly bug.

"I use my big fluttery wings to fly away from birds, high up in the sky..."

Up, up, and away!

"like this!" said the shiny blue bug.

Whoooooooooooooooooossshhh!

"Hmm," thought the very ugly bug.

"If only I had teeny tiny eyes, a smooth green back, and lovely

fluttery wings, then I would be safe from birds, too.

So the very ugly bug decided that she would make a mask to help her eyes look teeny tiny.

She used a leaf
to make her back look
smooth and green.

She even found a
pair of fluttery
wings. "I'll be safe
from birds now!"
she said.

But she wasn't safe at all. The funny disguise made her stand out even more! Now everyone could see her—including a big, hungry bird in the sky.

Ta-da!

"Yum, yum," said the bird. "Look at that lovely juicy bug down there. It looks delicious!" And he flew down for a tasty bug snack.

"Argh!" yelled the very ugly bug as the bird swooped closer. The other bugs quickly hid and flew away. Then, suddenly, something very strange happened.

The big scare made the very ugly bug even uglier.

Her big googly eyes got bigger.

Her lumpy head began to wiggle and wobble.

Her horrible hairy back spiked up,

and her spotted purple legs waved in the air.

She looked hideous!

"Ugh," said the bird. "That bug doesn't look tasty at all! It will give me a tummy ache." And he flew off to look for a nice juicy caterpillar instead.

very ugly bug!"

cheered the other bugs. "She's so ugly she scared the bird away!"

"Now I love the way I look!" said the very ugly bug proudly. And Mr. Ugly Bug agreed. He thought she was gorgeous.

The two ugly bugs fell in love and had
a big family of baby bugs...

who were all even uglier than their parents!

Love Bugs